A VERMONT BASKETBALL STORY

FRED CERRATO

A VERMONT BASKETBALL STORY

iUniverse books may be ordered through booksellers or by contacting:

iUniverse
1663 Liberty Drive
Bloomington, IN 47403
www.iuniverse.com
844-349-9409

ISBN: 978-1-6632-3111-6 (sc)
ISBN: 978-1-6632-3110-9 (e)

Library of Congress Control Number: 2021922005

Print information available on the last page.

iUniverse rev. date: 11/05/2021

CHAPTER 1

Christmas week was bleak in Vermont. Piles of snow made walking treacherous. There wasn't much to do. It was 1959, and there were two television stations: WPTZ out of Plattsburgh, New York, which was located across Lake Champlain, and WCAX, which was in Burlington).

There weren't many TVs available on campus, so Paul Fiore had a radio in his room. At night, he would tune into the superstations that transmitted fifty thousand watts: WABC in New York, WKBW in Buffalo, and WLS in Chicago. They would keep him company during those lonely nights as they played the songs of Jerry Lee Lewis, Fats Domino, and Chuck Berry.

Paul glanced out of his room's window and watched the fluttering snowflakes. It would have been a romantic sight if he was warmly nestled in the arms of his sweetheart, but she was three hundred miles away and in New Jersey. He had been with her five days ago but then returned to campus.

Paul was a basketball star for Castle College's team in Vermont. The team would be playing at a holiday tournament in Maine from January 2–5. Standing at six feet, two inches, Paul weighed 180 pounds. He had blue eyes and black hair. He had long arms, long fingers, and big hands. He was long and lanky. He was quick and fast on the basketball court, and he could easily touch the rim with a running start. He could palm the ball with his long hands and fingers. Opponents rarely stole the ball from Paul. He had a perfect basketball-player's body.

Paul had needed to return to college by December 27 to resume practice. It would be grueling three-hour sessions, once in the morning and once at night. None of the players were happy with this arrangement.

The only people on the Castle College campus during the holidays were the basketball players. These ten young men were unequally dispersed among four dormitories. There were no more than four players in each dorm. The practices were dreadful—three hours of running, running, and more running. By the end of it, they were so sapped of strength, they had to go back to the dorm for naps.

Tonight was New Year's Eve, and the coach gave the players a break: only one three-hour practice in the morning. Seven of the players had dates for that night and planned to have a wild New Year's Eve party in a nearby motel. Five others planned to go to town and make the rounds of the bars that night. Two others had no plans. Paul was one of the two, and the other was Luke Tate, who was a Vermont basketball standout. Luke was six feet, seven inches, and he weighed 240 pounds. His most outstanding trait was his hands. They were enormous. He used his hands to seemingly pluck rebounds out of thin air.

It was now 7:00 p.m. on December 31, 1959, and most of the guys had left either to pick up their dates or hit the bars. Once again, Paul glanced out the window. There was another dormitory adjacent to his, and he noticed that Luke's light was still on. He pondered whether he should walk over. At least then he wouldn't be alone, and they could usher in the new year together. Instead, Paul leaned back so that his chair became delicately balanced on its two hind legs. He reached over and clicked on the new clock radio that his parents had given him for Christmas.

In contrast to the desolation that he felt on campus, he had been celebrating Christmas at home one week earlier. Christmas was one of his favorite holidays. On Christmas Eve, the family had gathered at Aunt Angie's for the traditional Feast of the Seven Fishes. Each family brought a fish entree to the gathering. They dined on *baccala*, *scungille*, clams, scallops, shrimp, mussels, and flounder. After the repast, they attended Midnight Mass.

On Christmas morning, the family was up early and met at the Fiore's house to prepare the Christmas meal. Paul and his family lived in a small Cape Cod cottage in Glendale, New Jersey.

The women prepared homemade ravioli by rolling out the dough into thin strips and filling the strips with seasoned ricotta. They prepared *ragu* sauce by combining tomatoes, onions, garlic, parsley, and meats. It simmered for hours and filled the house with mouthwatering aromas.

The men were responsible for the antipasto and meat entrees. Paul's dad, Frank, and the rest of his uncles prepared the antipasto and grilled the filet mignon on charcoal grills in the driveway. Christmas presents were exchanged before dinner. The meal was a raucous affair with laughter, singing, and love of the family that was gathered together.

Paul now became unusually restless. Luke's light was still flickering through the sheet of snow, and it seemed to beckon him. He climbed into his all-purpose weatherproof winter boots, threw on his coat, and zipped his wool-lined hood over his head.

As he stepped out of his dormitory, the snow caked on his eyebrows. The subzero temperature caused the hair in his nostrils to freeze solid. It had been snowing several hours, and some of the snowdrifts were already as high as Paul's knees. Through winced eyes, he groped along as the snow overwhelmed him.

As he entered Luke's dorm, he threw back his hood and exposed his head. He was gratified by the welcome change in temperature as the heat permeated his body with a tingly sensation.

Paul hesitated while unfastening his coat because he could hear "Auld Lang Syne" quietly echoing from Luke's room. He thought that Luke was also lonely as he climbed the flight of stairs to the second floor.

CHAPTER 2

Luke's door was ajar. Paul approached and entered his room.

"Hey, Paul. How come you ain't out with the guys?"

Two cliques existed in the ball club. Neither Paul nor Luke were members of them. Both of them were sophomores, and the other team members were upper classmen. It would take time for them to be assimilated into the group. Paul and Luke were both great players, and they had earned the respect of their teammates.

"Nobody really asked me, Luke. Where are you going tonight?"

"Well, I was thinking of hitching a ride to Burlington to see my girl, but it's snowing too hard now. I was just leaving to walk downtown to get a few drinks. Why don't you come?"

Paul thought for a second and then spoke. "But I don't have any ID, and we aren't old enough to drink. How are we going to get served?"

Luke reached into his drawer and pulled out an ID card, a driver's license,

and a draft card. The items were the work of students who specialized in forgery for the implicit purpose of getting served.

"My roommate forgot his ID, and I've got my own. You can use his if you want. Those hicks downtown never know the difference. They never check real careful."

Prior to college, Paul rarely drank except for some wine at Sunday dinner. Paul was very naive. He knew a lot about basketball but not much about drugs, sex, or alcohol. Being a college student, he was learning quickly. He was acquiring a taste for beer and enjoyed going out and socializing with the guys. He could never understand why someone would drink alone solely for the sake of getting drunk. In college, he saw more and more of this type of behavior. In fact, he knew for certain that several of the seniors were alcoholics. Drinking was now beyond their control. Paul's thoughts were interrupted by Luke' prodding.

"Well, Paul, what do you say?"

"Okay, Luke. I can't take this damn place, especially tonight. We're going to have a helluva time getting downtown in this snow."

Luke gave Paul an assuring look. "You clowns from Jersey make me laugh. You just stay right behind me, and we'll get to town fine. I'm a veteran of eighteen Vermont snowbound winters."

Luke finished putting on his winter garb and handed Paul his fake ID. Paul gazed at his forged items and was amazed at how professional they looked.

As the two young men stepped out of the dormitory, Paul followed Luke's advice and let him lead the way. The hideous wind swirled the snow into whirlpools. It had completely covered the tracks that Paul had made earlier. Its pelting assault stubbornly fought the two young men. The campus was situated on a plateau. This elevation caused a normal snowstorm to reach blizzard proportions.

Luke used the flickering lampposts' lights as a guide, and soon, Paul could hear the chain-clanging tires of the automobiles on the highway, which was adjacent to the college. Their only hope of getting into town was to hitch a ride. If they tried to walk, it would take them an hour, and then they would probably need to have their frostbitten noses amputated.

The screaming wind made talk useless as a means of communication. The two abominable snowmen stood helplessly on the shoulder of the highway and extended mittened thumbs. Selfishly, Paul stepped in back of Luke and used him as a shield against the malevolent white cascade.

Paul could discern the quiet clang of chains and two searching, dot-like lights approaching from a distance. The two snowmen became animated and extended their snowbound arms as far as horizontally possible and waved them in classic hitchhiker fashion. They no longer felt the snow or wind but heard only the approaching clanging voice and brightening orbs of the auto.

As the 1948 Nash skidded to a halt, Luke ran over, quickly opened the door, and peered inside at the driver. "Goin' to Castleport Center?"

The driver and his automobile were stark contrasts to the pure, clean snow. Dirt and grime enveloped the dashboard and the ripped upholstery. With a quick smile and gesture, the driver beckoned them into the warm interior.

Luke continued to speak. "We're going to The Mill, so you can leave us off anywhere in Castleport."

The young driver nodded and smiled again. He then focused his entire attention to his archaic vehicle. He forced the clutch to the floorboard, sadistically grinding the gears. Suddenly, the Nash bucked and swerved into motion. The storm became much more sedate as they left the Castle College plateau and descended to the valley and Castleport.

As they neared Castleport, the driver talked over the whine of the transmission. "Are you guys on Castle College's basketball team?"

They both replied that they were. The driver continued. "I used to be a fanatic for the game. I couldn't get enough of it. When I was a sophomore in high school, I tried out for the basketball team. When I went up for a rebound, someone submarined me, and I crashed to the floor, breaking my hip and my leg in three places. My leg and my hip were not set correctly, and I ended up with a limp. The coach cut me, of course, and he wouldn't even let me be team manager. He was a real prick. People have made fun of me my whole life and called me gimp. Because of that incident during practice, I loathe basketball. I can't even watch it anymore."

"Sorry about what happened, Pal," said Luke.

"Could you let us off down the block? There's The Mill. We really appreciate the lift."

The driver leered at the two players as they left the car.

CHAPTER 3

During the early twentieth century, mills were prevalent along the Winooski River. The mills were responsible for much manufacturing: flour, yarn, paper, and linseed oil, among others. In 1927, a major flood destroyed many of the mills. All of the mills closed in 1954, but some of them were refurbished as restaurants, retail establishments, and bars.

As Paul and Tate entered The Mill, they immediately saw Jacques (Jack) Trapper Bonnet. He was sitting at a table with a group of townspeople, and he beckoned the boys over to his table.

Jack Bonnet was a fixture at the Castle College home games. Castle College was an all-male school. The ROTC band entertained the fans during the game, but there were no cheerleaders. Jack Bonnet took up the slack by coming to games in a raccoon coat, yelling through a megaphone, and exciting the crowd with his antics. He earned the nickname Trapper because of the raccoon coat.

Jack was a raconteur. He loved to hold court, and he liked his beer. He could usually be found at The Mill, especially on the weekends, so it was no surprise that Jack was there on New Year's Eve. He was the team's unofficial historian because he had been attending the games for the last twenty years.

Jack effusively praised Paul and Luke as they sat down at the table. Jack was talking about the upcoming holiday tournament between Castle College, Colby, Saint Anselm, and the University of Maine, which would be held in Portland, Maine.

Paul looked across the room and caught the eye of a gorgeous blond, who was wearing a Champlain College sweatshirt. Standing next to her was an equally gorgeous brunette. He thought that he and Luke might be able to make a move before twelve. After all, it was New Year's Eve.

Jack made sure that Paul's and Luke's glasses were filled with beer all night long. The boys knew that they shouldn't overdo it because they had a morning practice on the following day. Their conversations with the townspeople were convivial and cordial. They thoroughly enjoyed the evening. Jack offered to drive the boys back to college.

Twelve o'clock rolled around. The boys looked for the two young ladies from Champlain College, but alas, they were nowhere to be found.

Jack pulled up in his new 1959 Cadillac Coupe de Ville, complete with fins. The boys hopped in. With raised eyebrows, Paul and Luke looked at each other. They thought that it was a mighty nice car for a manager at Sears to have. The leather was plush, and the inside was cavernous. As they rode along, Beethoven's Ninth Symphony was playing on the concert-quality stereo. It was smooth sailing back to campus.

CHAPTER 4

George Calzoni was not only the coach of Castle College's basketball team but also the athletic director. The college allowed him several perks as athletic director. He, his wife, and his daughter received free housing in a handsome colonial-style home in an upscale neighborhood close to the campus. He also had a company car: a new 1959 Chevy Impala.

Coach Calzoni was fifty years old. He had an engaging smile, brown eyes, a hooked nose, and a bald pate. At six feet, four inches, he was tall and lanky. He liked to smoke long Phillip Morris Commanders cigarettes, and he had a ulcer. Nevertheless, he diligently exercised to keep himself in the best shape possible.

Calzoni was a respected member of the New England coaching community. He had coached for twenty-five years. He had seen the game of basketball change from a tedious athletic event where there was a jump ball after every basket to an exciting fast-paced sport which excited its rabid fans.

Calzoni was a great coach, but he was old-school. He was a disciplinarian, but he was fair. His practices were at least three hours long, where it was run, run, run. It was drills and repetition until the set plays became part of the players' essences. The practices were grueling.

He wanted his players to be in shape. He knew that some of his players were smokers and drinkers. He didn't care as long as they could play the whole game without getting winded. Coach believed in playing his five best players, so he wanted them to have some juice left at the end of the game.

This was the last practice before leaving for the holiday tournament in Portland, Maine. He had called a practice for that morning so that in the afternoon and evening, the players could rest and pack for the coming trip.

Coach Calzoni was very confident about the rest of the season. They had already won three games, and he felt that his team was loaded with talent. Because Castle College was a Division II school. They always competed in Division II programs. Calzoni was always able to recruit good players every year. He had a pipeline to New York's and New Jersey's metropolitan areas, where former players and alumni acted as scouts. They recruited all-star players and offered them full scholarships.

Paul Fiore had received his scholarship because a former Castle College player had recruited him. He had never heard of the Vermont school, but he became very interested when the former player said that Calzoni needed a guard and that Fiori would receive a full scholarship.

During the forties and fifties, many men who had fought in World War II and the Korean War had gone to Castle College on the GI Bill. Many of them were now Calzoni's scouts. They funneled many players from the metropolitan area up to Vermont. Castle College became a powerhouse in Division II basketball in New England. They had a bandbox for a gym on campus, but they played their games at the Burlington Memorial Auditorium in Vermont. The games were always packed.

Calzoni checked his clipboard. He wanted to make sure that he had covered all the important details during practice. If his team could remain injury free, he felt that this might be the year that they won a championship. However, unforeseen events could always ruin a season.

Calzoni scanned the gym and took an inventory of his players.

Hayes Aldridge was their six-feet-eleven-inch, all-American center. He had earned that accolade during the previous year when he had averaged over thirty points per game. He was also an academic All-American. He was a math major, and he had a 4.0 grade-point average.

Paul Fiore was a capable guard who had great ball-handling skills and an accurate shot. He improved as the year progressed.

Frank Balboni was the other guard. He was deadly at long range with a two-handed set shot. Wally Beemer and Luke Tate were excellent rebounders and jump shooters.

Coach Calzoni marveled at his wealth of talent. He also had very capable players who could come off the bench and relieve the starters. Johnny White, who was six feet, ten inches, was at the center position. Joe Biasi was at guard. Nat Parro, Bart Eclair, and Willy Crenna rounded out the team. They were seven players who were deep with talent.

Calzoni's assistant coach, Joe Mackey, was running some final drills that would conclude the practice. Then the players would shower, have lunch and dinner, pack, get a good night's sleep, and be ready to leave for Portland, Maine, in the morning.

Harry's Barbershop was a busy gathering place on Church Street in Burlington, Vermont. Politicians, athletes, and common folk got their haircuts there and offered the latest scandalous news and gossip of the day. Often, the men that frequented Harry's Barbershop did not get a haircut, but they hung around and talked about sports.

The hot topic was Castle College's basketball team and its recent win against Dartmouth. They had come from behind for an exciting win. Their first three games were creating a lot of buzz in Burlington.

The proprietor of the barbershop, Harry Casey, was of medium height with slicked-back hair and a mustache. He was dressed neatly in a blue dress shirt and dark-gray slacks. His barber's paraphernalia was spread out on a ledge beneath a massive mirror.

He was administering a tomahawk cut to a six foot eleven inch giant, who was quietly dozing in the barber's chair. The giant was

12

center for the Castle College basketball team. Stuffed in the barber's chair with legs and arms akimbo, the giant appeared clumsy, but on the basketball court, he exhibited the grace of a ballet dancer.

When the haircut was finished, Harry Casey nudged Hayes Aldridge and said, "The haircut's done. Wake up."

"Thanks, Harry. I thought I'd get a haircut after our morning practice. Sorry I dozed off, but practice tired me out. We're leaving for the holiday tournament tomorrow morning."

"I know. Nat Parro was in earlier, and he said the coach really worked you hard," said Casey.

"What do I owe you?" asked Aldridge.

"Hayes, don't worry about it. It's on the house. Just make sure you score thirty against Maine. I have a few bucks bet on the game. In fact, there's been a lot of talk about your team's first three games, and we've had some friendly wagering here in the shop."

Hayes looked at Harry. "Harry, I want to pay you for the haircut."

"Don't worry about it. It's on me."

"Thanks, Harry, but the next time, I'm paying."

"It's a deal, Hayes. What you don't realize is that you're a star and you are bringing in customers for me."

Harry Casey had a big portrait on his wall of Hayes with his All State trophy. He was shaking Harry's hand. Hayes had been named to the Small College All America First Team during the previous season.

"I don't think the coach is going to appreciate my tomahawk haircut, but what's he going to do, bench me?"

CHAPTER 5

The morning came for the trip to Portland, Maine. Coach Cal wanted to make sure that everyone was ready on time, so he called for everyone to shape up an hour before departure. Departure would be at 9:00 a.m., but Cal wanted everyone outside Founders Hall at 8:00 a.m. His hurry-up-and-wait tactic was to ensure that there were no stragglers.

Castle College was the only college in America that did not travel to away games in a bus. To save money, Calzoni, as athletic director, sent the team and any ancillary personnel to away games in two limousines. One was a Cadillac, and the other was a Chrysler. This was much cheaper way than renting a bus.

The two limousines pulled up and stopped in front of Founders Hall. The proprietor of the limousine company was Deniz Memet, and the name of the company was Memet Inc. Deniz drove the Cadillac, and his brother, Emre, drove the Chrysler.

Memet Deniz was from Turkey. He had immigrated many years earlier to Burlington, Vermont, where he started a taxi service. Both of Memet's cars were very modern and updated with technology of the day. Both cars were outfitted with snow tires, which were relatively rare on most cars in 1960. Most cars in New England were outfitted with chains to get them through the snowy winters.

Memet Deniz was called Dennis by the players, and Emre was called Henry. Dennis and Henry were very good drivers, especially when it snowed, which happened often on road trips. Both Dennis and Henry knew how to navigate their two behemoth limousines through swirling snowflakes.

Because it had folding seats, the Cadillac seated ten; however, it was cramped because the players were so tall. Most of the players rode in the Cadillac. Coaches, managers, a team doctor, a statistician, and special guests went in the Chrysler.

In the Chrysler, Calzoni held court while smoking and drinking a carton of milk, which his doctor said would calm his ulcer. In the Cadillac, Wally Beemer, Bart Eclair, and Joe Biasi bummed Marlboros from each other. There was no escape from the smoke in either car. Will Crenna sat in the front seat and took care of the radio. When some of the players fell asleep, their heads lolled and drool ran down their chins. It was not a pleasant ride.

Coach George Calzoni was an insomniac. If he got four hours of sleep, he was lucky. He had a routine on road trips. After they had arrived at their destination, eaten, and gotten settled, Calzoni would hang out in the hotel lobby late into the night and long after the players were in their rooms.

Coach Cal knew everyone. He had been in the minors with Casey Stengel. During the summer, he worked at basketball camps with NBA players like Dolph Schayes and Bob Cousy. He had friends all over the coaching spectrum.

One example of Cal's status in the coaching community took place during Paul Fiore's freshman year. The Celtics played the Lakers in a preseason exhibition game at Burlington Memorial Auditorium. Coach Cal had all upper-class ballplayers go into the Celtics locker room for a meet and greet. Cal had been an instructor at Red Auerbach's summer basketball camp, and they were good friends. Imagine the thrill of meeting those basketball icons. Paul was not on the varsity team, so he had to be content with just watching the game.

Paul had never seen pro-basketball players in person. He was enthralled as he watched the hulking giants warm up for the game.

He could not help but marvel at the grace that these giants displayed as they completed their warm-ups.

During the game, he watched his idol Bob Cousy destroy the Laker guards with his behind-the-back dribble and no-look passes. Bill Russell intimidated any player who dwelled into his zone. He glared at and dared them to take a shot, which he then blocked to one of his teammates. Elgin Baylor soared through the air, scoring one fadeaway jump shot after another. He would also hang in the air, do a 360, and slam the ball through the hoop. Paul had never seen such quality of play.

Whenever Cal was in town, his cronies would visit him at the hotel. If the team was playing Holy Cross in Worcester, Massachusetts, Cal might be in the lobby with Tommy Heinsohn, Cousy, or Sharman. They would stay up most of the night rehashing war stories. Even though Calzoni was an insomniac with an ulcer, he couldn't help but admit that he loved those road trips.

The limousines were ready for their journey to Portland, Maine. Coach Cal eyed Hayes Aldridge. "What's with the haircut? If you don't average thirty-five points, fifteen rebounds, and four blocked shots, I'm personally going to shave your head!" Then they were on their way.

CHAPTER 6

When the team arrived at Eastland Hotel in Portland, they all disembarked and retrieved their luggage. Paul followed Nat Parro into the lobby. Nat had a tendency of getting a bit carsick on trips. Nat put his right hand on his stomach. "You know, Paul, my stomach feels a bit queasy. I think I need a little Drambuie to calm it down."

"Nat, have you ever heard of Pepto Bismol? If Coach Cal sees you walking into the bar to buy liquor, he'll send you home."

"No, Pepto Bismol is not going to cut it. I need Drambuie."

Nat walked to the bar, which was in back of the lobby. Paul waved to Luke and walked away from Nat while shaking his head. Some of his teammates' quirks were hard to fathom.

On away games, Coach Calzoni assigned two players to a room except for Hayes Aldridge. Hayes was the star of the team, and he didn't want a roommate. The players on the team were okay with this setup. After all, Bill Russell didn't like to practice. Red Auerbach ran the Celtics ragged while Bill Russell sat in the stands and watched. Russell was so great that the rest of the team never complained. Castle College players never complained because Hayes Aldridge gave them thirty-two points, ten rebounds, and four blocked shots per game.

At the Eastman Hotel, Paul Fiore and Luke Tate were roommates. The accommodations were very good. The hotel was old but well-kept and clean.

After a good night's sleep, it was time for breakfast. Paul and Luke were famished and looking forward to a satisfying meal. Paul was not used to elegance. His parents could not afford to take him to high-end restaurants back in New Jersey, so he was impressed when he saw the dining room setup: white linen tablecloths, silver cutlery, and gold-plated place settings of tableware. Black waiters were elegantly dressed in tuxedos and wearing white gloves. Their neatly groomed white hair added to the ambiance. One of the waiters handed Paul and Luke their menus. "Take your time and look over the menus, gentlemen. Would you like some orange juice and coffee?"

Paul looked at the menu. "What is eggs Benedict?"

The waiter replied that it was a poached egg atop an English muffin that was covered in hollandaise sauce. "I highly recommend it," said the waiter. "And I also recommend the croissant with our wonderful Maine blueberry jam."

Paul said it sounded delicious, and Luke agreed. Breakfast was divine.

Some of the perks of being a college basketball player were staying in top hotels, experiencing new cuisines, and traveling to new locales all over the east coast. The players later learned that the elegant waiters had retired from the Pullman Car Company, which had regaled customers with fine dining and accommodations during the heyday of train travel.

Before going back to their room, Paul and Luke both picked up a copy of the *Portland Press Herald*. They sat, relaxed, and read them until it was time for the pregame meal at noon. The game would take place at four in the afternoon against the University of Maine. The game would be played at the Portland Exposition Building, which gave patrons a variety of venues: track and field, basketball, concerts, conferences, and civic meetings. The University of Maine didn't have one of the top teams in the tournament, so Castle College expected to put one in the win column that afternoon.

As the young men were relaxing in their room, Luke noted

something about an article. "I'm reading an interesting article about the mafia in Montreal."

"I didn't know they had a mafia in Montreal," answered Paul.

"Yes there is, and the head capo is Nicolo Rizzuto."

"You mean like Phil 'the Scooter' Rizzuto?"

"I don't think it's any relation. It says they're involved in drug trafficking, murder, loan-sharking, weapons, and illegal gambling; specifically fixing basketball games. That is scary. The mafia fixing basketball games? Do you think they would ever try to fix our games?"

"Listen. We're not Division 1 like Kentucky and North Carolina. We're small potatoes. Why would they waste their time on us? I'm not defending the mafia, but they're not responsible for all crime. I've read about the basketball scandals of the early 1950s, and the mafia had nothing to do with them. It was a gambler named Jack Molinas, who involved players from several New York City colleges.

"Players from Kentucky were also involved in another scandal, again with gamblers. The scandals ruined the players' lives. They could never play in any organized league again. Forget about the NBA. Many of them went to jail just for a little extra spending money to line their pockets. It's stupid! Besides, I don't understand anything about betting. I don't get it. I don't know what they're talking about: point spread, over under. Do you know what any of that shit means?"

"I don't get it, and I don't want anything to do with it. I just want to play basketball, pass my courses, and get my degree. Keep it simple," answered Luke.

Paul and Luke spent the rest of the morning reading, relaxing, and dozing. Finally it was noon and time for the pregame meal. It was going to be served in the hotel's dining room again, with silver service, gold-plated cutlery, and elegant waiters. The pregame meal was always the same: a steak, a baked potato, and green beans.

The game was scheduled for four o'clock, so they had ample time to digest their meals. Many college teams ate the same pregame meal, but some of the other colleges had other ideas. The coach of Colby College had his players eat pasta for their pregame meal. He thought that the carbs in pasta would give his players a boost during the games.

Sometimes on road trips, Coach Cal gave the players money so that they could get their own pregame meals In Boston when they were playing Northeastern, Paul and his teammate Will Crenna had no idea where they were or where they should go.

When they came upon a fish restaurant, they looked at the menu in the window. Paul's knowledge of fish was limited. His mother would fry smelts in garlic and vinegar, and his breath would stink for days. She also baked salt cod (*baccala*) with herbs. That was the extent of his knowledge.

Paul was unfamiliar with the array of fish on the menu: arctic char, sturgeon, *branzino*, and swordfish. Paul and Will opted for the swordfish, and they were not disappointed. It was ambrosia.

On another road trip to play Providence College in Road Island, the team ate at a restaurant that had a gigantic charcoal firepit, where porterhouse steaks were roasting on top of the grills. Patrons were allowed to select their steaks, and waiters would serve these at their tables. The steaks, which were a combination of New York strip steak and filet mignon, were very unctuous, tender, and tasty.

Today, they had another mundane sirloin, baked potato, and green beans. It was not a culinary adventure.

It was time to get ready for the game. Coach Calzoni was very strict about what players wore to the game. At a local clothing store in Burlington before the season began, all players were outfitted with blue blazers, light blue dress shirts, and gray slacks. There was never any question about the dress code. Their behavior and attire would be a positive representation of Castle College.

The team assembled in the locker room at 3:00 p.m. and got ready for the 4:00 p.m. tip-off. The team members clothed themselves in their uniforms. The team manager, Mike Tragussi, made sure that all the equipment was ready. The assistant coach, Joe Mackey, was ready to go over the scouting report.

In the early 1950s, Joe Mackey had been one of Coach Calzoni's players. Whenever Cal's ulcer acted up, Mackey took over his coaching responsibilities. As Cal aged, Mackey was often the coach. Mackey had an electric personality and an upbeat outlook. He attended coaching clinics all over the country, and he was well versed in the newest offenses and defenses of the day. He was a player's coach, and they loved him.

The team doctor, Dr. Jim Bombard, was also in attendance. He was a friend of Calzoni, and he had been with the team for many years. He was, however, a closet alcoholic, so it was up to Calzoni to make sure that he was sober for the game in case anyone needed medical attention. Thankfully, it was rare that anyone needed medical attention.

Mackey went over the scouting report in detail. He gave a comprehensive evaluation of the team's starting five and their offensive and defensive setup. The University of Maine had a 2-2 record against poor competition, so there was nothing much to worry about.

Calzoni gave his standard pregame spiel: start strong, do not to let up, have your hands up on defense, block out on rebounds, run the plays that they had practiced, and get back on the fast break.

The starting lineup was announced, although it never varied from these five players: Paul Fiore and Frank Balboni at guard, Wally Beeman and Luke Tate at forward, and Hayes Aldridge at center. The players all formed a circle, gave their pregame whoop, and ran onto the court to do their warm-ups and lay-up drills.

Castle College dominated from the start and won by twenty-five points. Hayes Aldridge was unstoppable. He had developed ambidexterity, and he scored easily. He was quick and used a head fake to get a step on his opponent and go left or right to get to the hoop. He could hit from near or far with a deadly jump shot. He developed a baby hook close to the basket, along with his patented slam dunk. His stat line for the game was thirty-six points, fifteen rebounds, and four blocked shots.

His teammates also had a field day. Balboni made a deadly two-handed set shot, anywhere from twenty-to-thirty feet away from the basket. He made six shots in a row and ended up with nineteen points. Beemer was a great rebounder, although he was not a high jumper. He knew how to score around the basket: off rebounds and on tap-ins and put-backs. Basketball aficionados called it garbage. He also made deadly jump shots from the corner. Beemer ended up with fifteen points.

Fiore's job as playmaker was to set up the plays and hit the open man. When he was in the clear, he would shoot the ball. He had a change of pace and used a spin move to the hoop. He developed a one-hand set shot that he could take on the run off the dribble like his idol Bob Cousy. He ended up with eleven points and eight assists.

Luke Tate rounded out the scoring with ten. Saint Anselm defeated Colby College in the nightcap. It would be Castle College against Saint Anselm on the following day for the championship of the tournament.

CHAPTER 7

The day of the championship game was a total replica of the day before. Paul and Luke walked to the arena. As they were crossing the street to go to the Exposition Center, Luke looked ahead and elbowed Paul.

"Why are you elbowing me? Are you sharpening your elbows for the game?"

"Look down the street, Paul. Isn't that the car that picked us up on New Year's Eve at the college?"

"It can't be. There's no way that bucket of bolts could make it all the way from Burlington to Portland."

They arrived at the arena and got ready for the game. The mood in the locker room was somber and tense. Castle College would have to be at the top of their game to win.

Calzoni surveyed the locker room. "Where's Aldridge?"

The players looked around the room and at each other. Some shrugged their shoulders.

Nat Parro piped up. "I saw him go into his room after the pregame meal."

Willy Crenna added, "I know he likes to have a cup of herbal tea before the game. It helps him to relax."

"Has anyone seen him since then?" Calzoni's ulcer was starting to percolate. "We have a game in an hour. Where is he?" There was still no response from anyone on the team. Calzoni looked at the team manager. "Mike, could you look inside the gym? See if you can find him. Take a walk outside too."

The players were all dressed when Mike returned ten minutes later. "Coach, he isn't anywhere. I looked inside and outside the building."

"Jeez, where can he be? Did anyone see him leave his room?" There was still no response from the players. "Now I'm getting worried. Maybe he tripped in his room and hit his head. We have to get somebody over there. Sorry to do this to you again, Mike, but could you run over to the hotel? I'll give you a note that allows you to check his room if it's locked."

Mike sprinted to the hotel and explained the situation to the concierge in the lobby. A manager accompanied Mike up to Aldridge's room. He unlocked the door and found the room vacant. Mike sprinted back to the arena as the game was about to start. "Coach, he's not in his room. No one has seen him."

"Holy God. What the hell is going on? I'm responsible for the kid! Where could he be? This is what I get for letting him room alone." Calzoni looked at his assistant coach, Joe Mackey.

"Joe, what should we do?"

"Send Mike back to the hotel. Have him look around the area and ask some questions. We'll deal with it after the game. We have to play the game.

"Mike, is that okay with you? I know I have you running around like a rabbit, but I'm very worried."

"No problem, Coach. I'll go right now."

"Let me know immediately if you find out anything."

Mike went back to the hotel, sat in the lobby, and then made a tour of the surrounding neighborhood. When he finished his tour, he went back to the lobby, hoping that Hayes would appear.

Castle College simply could not compete with Saint Anselm College without Hayes Aldridge. Johnny White, Hayes's replacement could not duplicate Hayes's stat line, and the team lost by fifteen points.

After the game, the players were deafeningly silent. They were despondent about the game and having their teammate literally disappear.

At seven o'clock, Hayes Aldridge walked into Eastland Hotel's lobby. Mike Tragussi jumped up as if a firecracker had been under his butt. "Where have you been? Everybody's worried about you! The coach was so upset that I thought he was going to have a stroke."

Hayes sank down on one of the lobby's comfortable leather sofas. "After the pregame meal, I went back to my room and ordered a chamomile tea. I relaxed for a while, and then I went out for a little walk. That's my usual routine before an away game. I started to feel very drowsy and disoriented, so I sat down on a park bench. After a minute, I was out. I woke up, and it was dark out. I still felt woozy, but I thought that I should get back to the hotel. Just let me sit here. I still feel drowsy."

Mike sprinted back to the arena. He was getting a workout.

The players were filing out as he bolted into the locker room. He ran over to Calzoni. "Hayes is in the lobby of the hotel. He just walked in," he yelled.

Calzoni sank into a folding chair and exhaled a sigh of relief. "Did you hear that guys. Hayes is okay. Is he okay? Did he say what happened?"

The players' somber demeanors changed to jubilation at the news of Hayes's return. Mike repeated Hayes's story of what had happened as they all left the room.

Calzoni and Coach Mackey hurried over to the Eastland Hotel. They hurried up to Aldridge's room. The door was unlocked, and Hayes was resting on the bed. Calzoni was overcome with emotion and relief. "How are you? Are you okay? Mike told us what happened. I thought the worst. I thought you were kidnapped. I have so much agita that my ulcer is screaming! Why do you think you blacked out?"

"Like I told Mike, after I had the pregame meal, I went back to my room and ordered a chamomile tea from room service. It relaxes me before a game. I was getting a little restless with pregame butterflies, so I went out for a walk. I started to feel a little woozy, so I sat on a park bench. That's all I remember until I woke up. It was dark, and I was disoriented and tired. I went back to the hotel and saw Mike in the lobby."

"Do you think you had food poisoning or some kind of bug or virus? What could have caused you to black out like that?"

"I don't know, Coach. I'm sorry I wasn't there for the game."

"Don't worry about that, son. The important thing is that we found you and that you're okay. Listen, I think you should be checked out by a doctor. Maybe we could have Dr. Bombard examine you." Joe Mackey gave Calzone an incredulous look. "On second thought, maybe we'll wait until we get back to Burlington to have a doctor check you out."

"A much better idea," said Mackey.

"Listen, Hayes, from now on, you will have a roommate for all road trips. We're going to keep an eye on you. We're going back to campus tonight, and you are going to travel with me. Pack up your things and be ready in an hour. And another thing. The newspapers are going to go berserk about this. I do not want you to talk to any reporters. All questions should be directed to me. I will tell them what happened. Do you understand?"

"Okay, Coach," responded Hayes.

As Calzoni and Mackey left the room, Calzoni commented to Mackey, "I'm really worried about that kid. People who have brain tumors black out like that. We've got to get him to a doctor, and quick!"

Hayes was part of the Calzoni entourage on the way home. He slept the entire trip.

Detective Pete Christos was surveying his notes at the Detective Services Bureau (DSB) in Burlington, Vermont. He had an unkempt appearance. He wore a rumpled suit, and his tie was askew. His parted black hair was plastered down with Vaseline Hair Tonic. He hadn't shaved in several days as evidenced by the stubble on his face and chin. Detective Christos had worked for the DSB for fifteen years. He was well respected for his thoroughness and intelligence. He carefully filled the bowl of his pipe with aromatic apple pipe tobacco. He lit it with his Zippo lighter and puffed until the room was filled with fragrant smoke. The pipe relaxed and helped him to concentrate.

Detective Christos had recently received correspondence from the F.B.I. in Boston who were investigating a syndicate that was involved in point shaving in sporting events, particularly basketball. The FBI had sent correspondence to all police forces in New England to ask for their assistance.

As Christos pondered the correspondence, he thought of Hayes Aldridge's mysterious disappearance in Maine. Although Aldridge had finally appeared, what had caused his disappearance wasn't clear. Detective Christos felt there were a lot of questions that needed to be answered. He thought he might want to question Aldridge sometime in the future.

He thoughtfully puffed his pipe as he gathered his notes so that he could head home for a relaxing dinner. The pipe tobacco's apple aroma wafted after him as he left the building.

CHAPTER 8

The headline on the front page of the *Burlington Free Press* read, "ALDRIDGE AWOL." The article detailed the disappearance of Hayes Aldridge during the Saint Anselm championship game. The editorial page opined conjecture and conspiracy theories. The paper promised readers an interview with Coach Calzoni.

Calzoni read the newspaper in his office, along with Joe Mackey. "I knew the paper would have a field day with this story. Joe, I don't want you to say anything about what happened. All inquiries should come to me. Also, I'm going to call my personal physician, Dr. Rameesh Patel, over at Fanny Allen Hospital and make an appointment to have Aldridge examined. In fact, I'm going to call him now." He asked his secretary to get Dr. Patel on the line.

"Dr. Patel, this is George Calzoni over at Castle College. I'd like to schedule one of my players, Hayes Aldridge, for a comprehensive exam. I'd like a complete workup, Doctor—soup to nuts—pardon the pun."

"Very funny," replied Dr. Patel.

"I'm not trying to be funny, Doctor. I'm trying to be thorough. I'd like a full examination, X-rays, or whatever it takes. I don't know if you read the article in the *Burlington Free Press*, but Hayes blacked out for several hours. I'm concerned that it's something very serious like a brain tumor."

"Let's not jump to conclusions. It could be many other things."

"That's why I want to get him in there as quickly as possible. I talked to his parents this morning, and they're so concerned that they want to make a special trip up from New Jersey. I just want to put their minds at ease." Dr. Patel said that he would be able to schedule a comprehensive exam for the following day.

Hayes underwent a battery of tests at Fanny Allen Hospital. Dr. Patel called Calzoni after the tests were completed. "Good news, Coach. Hayes Aldridge is in excellent health. The tests indicated no viruses or bacteria. We took X-rays. We even did a brain scan. There was no indication of any tumor or cranial problems. He can participate in all normal activities and resume practice."

"Thank you, Doctor. I'm very relieved, but I still don't understand why he blacked out. What could have caused it?"

"All tests proved negative. Sometimes food allergies can cause adverse reactions. Maybe he ate some bad food that only affected him. Food allergies could cause your blood pressure to plummet and result in fainting or blackouts, but it is very difficult to determine the cause of the food allergy unless it happens repeatedly."

"Well thanks again, Doc. I really appreciate it. I'm going to call his parents immediately with the good news. Thank everybody over there at Fanny Allen Hospital for their help."

CHAPTER 9

The students were returning to the Castle College campus after the Christmas break. There was a return to normalcy on campus. Classes resumed, and there were no more double-session practices for Fiore.

Paul Fiore's roommate, Barry Gleason, returned with a new car. It was an Edsel that his parents had purchased for him over the Christmas holiday. Paul and Barry could ride around Castleport and Burlington in style.

As classes resumed, there was mounting pressure on Paul. He was a business major, and he was having some difficulty with his courses. Coach Calzoni provided tutors to any player that needed special help. Most of Paul's grades were in the C or D range. Terms like *accounts receivable*, *debits*, and *credits* were foreign to him. Tutors were helping somewhat, but he just didn't get it. He had to maintain a certain grade-point average, or he would be ineligible to play.

He was also under pressure from his girlfriend, Lauren, back in New Jersey. They corresponded several times a week, and if he waited too long to respond, she complained. When Paul received the dreaded Dear John letter, he was relieved.

Paul also wrote to his parents weekly. He kept them up on current events by sending them clippings from the *Burlington Free Press* about the games.

With classes, practices, games, and letter writing, it was overwhelming. Paul had enough to deal with keeping up with his studies and what was happening on the basketball court. What was happening with his girlfriend's social life only complicated the situation.

They had said that they loved each other, but as Paul became more and more busy with all his activities, he thought of her less and less. She wanted to go out with her friends and have fun. Lauren was a very pretty and vivacious young lady. She didn't want to feel that she was cheating, hence the letter. The arrangement was that they could date other people, but if they chose to see each other when Paul was home, they could. Their correspondence, however, would stop. Paul wrote back one last time and stated that this new arrangement was better for both of them.

Castle College went on a winning streak. The players were learning each other's moves and continued to improve. Hayes Aldridge was magnificent. The other big man, Johnny White, was also improving his game. He was a 6'10" replacement for Aldridge, and his improvement allowed Coach Calzoni to substitute for Aldridge during the game making the rested Aldridge even more effective.

Castle College defeated Middlebury, Hartford, Bryant, and the University of New Hampshire. Their record was 8-1. If it wasn't for that debacle in Maine, they would have been undefeated.

Their next game was an away game against Norwich University in Norwich, Vermont. Norwich was a military school, and they had a very good team. It would be another test for Castle College because it would be on their court.

Hayes Aldridge was no longer rooming alone on road trips. His new roommate was Johnny White, and they got along fine. Hayes was like a mentor. He schooled White on all aspects of the game.

The team was staying at the Norwich Inn. Since the game would start at 8:00 p.m., the team would stay overnight and leave early the next morning. Usually the team had its pregame meal together, but Calzoni decided to give the players meal money and let them have dinner on their own. Willy Crenna, Nat Parro, Luke Tate, Johnny

White, Hayes Aldridge, and Paul Fiore decided to go out to dinner together.

They went to a pub close to the Norwich Inn. They all sat down at a large table, and they were given menus. When the waiter took their drink orders, most of the players chose Coca-Cola or 7Up.

When the waiter asked Aldridge for his drink order, he said, "I'll have a Heineken."

Paul, who was usually quiet, was infuriated. "What do you mean you'll have a Heineken? We have a game in a couple of hours."

"I feel like having a beer," answered Aldridge.

"I know you're the star of the team and think you're infallible, but you can't be at the top of your game if you're having a pregame beer. Besides, we're on a winning streak. We're really getting into a groove—a good rhythm. Do you want to jeopardize that?"

"Listen. I'm a senior. I'm twenty-one. I feel like having a beer. It's not going to affect me or the team. You'll see."

"I think you're being an asshole," answered Paul.

None of the other players responded, and the meal was eaten in silence. When the players were ready for dessert, Aldridge called over the waiter. "I'll have another Heineken," which made Paul exasperated.

During the game, Aldridge was lethargic. He tried to make moves to the basket, but he knocked the ball out of bounds with his foot. He scored from close in, but his jump shots were bricks clanging off the rim. He had trouble blocking out and elevating for rebounds. The pregame beer was affecting his game.

Near the end of the game, his stat line was eleven points and three rebounds. With a minute left in the game, Norwich was ahead by two points (seventy to sixty-eight). Usually the team would go to Aldridge if the game was close, but he was clearly having an off night.

With thirty seconds left in the game, Balboni tied the score with a long two-handed set shot. Norwich came down the court and began a weave in an attempt to stall and wait for the last shot.

Ten seconds were left when Paul Fiore stole the ball. He saw Tate streaking down the left side of the lane toward Castle College's basket. Fiore hooked him a long down-court pass, which Tate converted into the winning basket as time ran out. The final score was Castle College seventy-two and Norwich seventy. Castle College had survived, no thanks to Hayes Aldridge.

After the game, Calzoni made the rounds in the locker room, congratulating the players. He went over to where Fiore and Tate were getting dressed. "Great game, fellas. That was close. You really saved our ass. That was great defense, Paul. You were really up on that guy. He lost his concentration, and you knocked the ball away. That's how you win ball games: by exploiting the other team's errors. Great job. Great pass to Luke. Luke, great instincts to race down the court toward our basket. Those are qualities that are innate. They can't be taught, and I'm thankful that you had them tonight. Fantastic job!"

Calzoni walked over to Hayes Aldridge. "What happened tonight, Hayes? That was so unlike you."

"I don't know, Coach. Just an off night I guess," answered Aldridge.

"Everybody is entitled to an off night once in a while. The important thing is that we won the game and our mini streak is intact. You've been great all year. You'll bounce back the next game." Hayes Aldridge nodded, but he couldn't help feeling ashamed for having those pregame beers.

CHAPTER 10

The team, managers, coaches, and other people were up early the next morning for the trip back home. Hayes went back to the Cadillac limo. Paul asked Will Crenna if he could sit in the front seat and work the radio on the way home. Crenna said that was fine and sat in the back seat. The trip was relatively uneventful.

Some of the players were reading newspapers, and others were reading magazines. Joe Biasi was the intellectual one on the team. He was a math major and consistent Dean's List student. He did, however, like to read about strange phenomena like the Loch Ness Monster, the Abominable Snowman, and flying saucers. In fact, he was reading *Flying Saucer Magazine* when Nat Parro asked, "Are you reading about little green men from Mars?"

"No, I'm reading about little gray men. There's an article here about a flying saucer crashing in Roswell, New Mexico, in 1947. Debris from the crash was scattered over a large area, and there were several occupants inside the saucer. Supposedly, one of the occupants was still alive. The military took the occupants, debris, and flying saucer to one of its military bases.

At first, they said that a flying saucer had crash-landed, but the very next day, the army changed its tune and said that it was just weather balloons that had crashed."

Nat said, "I don't believe any of that nonsense. If they were really from another planet, the government would tell us."

"Well ever since 1947, thousands of people have been seeing strange phenomena in the sky. There was even a flap in 1952 when flying saucers flew over the White House."

"Are you kidding me?" Nat exclaimed.

"No, I'm not kidding. In fact, President Truman was so concerned that he created a special commission to study the flying saucer problem."

"I still don't believe it."

"Would it shock you to know that I saw one?"

"Now I know you're crazy. When did this happen?"

"Back in 1956 when I was still in high school, I had to get up early one day. It was about 6:30 a.m., and I happened to look out my kitchen window at the sky. There was low cloud cover with a gap between the clouds. Right below the clouds there was a shining, pulsating light. It looked like the brightest star I had ever seen. I stared at it for a couple of minutes because it was so bright and I didn't know what it was."

Everyone in the car was listening. "Suddenly, the object started to rise toward the gap in the clouds. It zigzagged through the gap in the clouds and disappeared."

"It was probably a helicopter," offered Nat.

"It wasn't a helicopter. It wasn't a bird. It wasn't a plane. It wasn't superman. I don't know what it was."

"I still don't believe it," Nat said.

"Nat, I want you to look at the sky tonight. All the stars that you see are suns just like our sun. Around those stars, there are planets. There are two hundred billion stars in our galaxy alone, and there are billions of galaxies. Do you really think that there is no intelligent life on any of those billions of planets? Don't you think that's absurd?"

"I think it's all bullshit. I think you made up that story. I think you're a kook. I don't believe any of it: flying saucers, little green men."

"In fact, at Roswell, the occupants were little gray men. They were about three-and-a-half-feet tall, with spindly arms, four fingers, large heads, and large black eyes."

"Sounds like Parro's last girlfriend," offered Bart Eclair.

"Sounds like your momma," said Parro.

"Boys, quiet!" Dennis, the driver, hardly ever said anything, but he wanted to get their attention. It was starting to snow. Dennis did not want to be distracted while he was driving. Snow squalls were making it difficult to see. Visibility was down to twenty yards, and the street was icing up. They were on Route 7 outside of Burlington, so they were almost home. The squalls were intensifying. Dennis was having a difficult time navigating the Cadillac over the icy road.

When Paul looked out the front window, he could barely see a pickup truck, which seemed to be careening toward them. The pickup truck was clearly out of control, and the limo was slipping and sliding. Paul soon realized there was no way that the two vehicles could avoid colliding.

Dennis uttered, *"Bok!"* Paul was certain that it was a Turkish curse word.

Paul was about to encounter one of the most bizarre experiences of his life. When he realized that the two vehicles could not avoid colliding as he looked at the careening pickup, time … slowed … down.

The truck should have hit the limo within seconds, but Paul observed that as it closed in on the limo, it went slower … and slower … and slower. When it was at its closest to the limo, it seemed to not be moving at all. Time was stretched as if someone was pulling on a rubber band. The space-time continuum was distorted.

"Crack!" As the two vehicles collided, it was as if that rubber band had snapped back into place and time had returned to normal.

Dennis pulled over to the side of the road, and the pickup truck's driver did the same. The Chrysler, which was following the Cadillac, also pulled over. The truck driver, Dennis, Dennis's brother Henry, Coach Calzoni, and Joe Mackey got out of their respective vehicles to assess the damage. Luckily, it was only minor issues for each vehicle. Dennis and the driver exchanged insurance information. Then they were on their way back to campus.

CHAPTER 11

Barry Gleason called to his roommate, "Hey, Paul, do you want to go out tonight? I'm dating a girl from UVM, and she has a friend."

"You mean a double date? A blind date?"

"Yeah, her friend is free tonight. She doesn't have a date."

"Barry, I've really been burned on blind dates. What's her weight? I don't want to go out with anyone heavier than me. I've gone out with some young ladies who were really *faccia brutta*. Do you know what that means in Italian? It means ugly!"

"Paul, I think you'll be pleasantly surprised. She's from Newport, which is in Northern Vermont and close to Quebec. She is very pretty. Her name is Connie Barbeau. She's French. She goes to Champlain College. My girlfriend, Corrine, and she went to high school together."

"Sounds very good, but I suspect some sugarcoating here."

"I'm not sugarcoating at all. We'll go to the drive-in movie in Burlington, and then we'll get a bite to eat at Stewart's."

"OK, Barry, but I don't want to get a hot dog and root beer at Stewart's. Let's go to Bove's and have some pasta."

"Bove's sounds even better." said Barry.

Barry and Paul picked up Corrine and Connie from Corrine's dorm, which was located at the University of Vermont. When Paul saw Connie, he was indeed pleasantly surprised. She was five feet, five inches and very shapely. She had hazel eyes and full lips. Her beautiful highlighted brown hair was cut in a short bob.

As they were driving to the drive-in, Paul and Connie became acquainted with each other. She was an education major, and she wanted to teach elementary school. Paul explained that he wasn't sure what he wanted to do after college. He talked about the pressures of being on the basketball team and keeping his grades up.

As they arrived at the drive-in, Paul said, "You know what? I think I've seen you someplace before, but I just can't put my finger on it."

"I was at The Mill on New Year's Eve. I saw you looking over at us."

"Oh, you were with the blond."

"Everyone remembers the blond, my friend Marilyn. She's stunning."

"I remembered you, didn't I?" said Paul.

"Yes you did. Marilyn is Jack Bonnet's niece. He drove us to The Mill that night, and we left early to go to a New Year's Eve party. You know Jack, don't you? He wears the raccoon coat and does all the cheering at the games."

"I know Jack well. He's a fixture at all the games. Sometimes I even see him at practice. I understand he's a manager at Sear's in Burlington. He drove Luke Tate and me back to the dorm in his gorgeous 1959 Cadillac de Ville. How can he afford that car on his salary?"

Connie answered, "Marilyn and I talked about that. He has that car and a beautiful house in Essex Junction, and he isn't married. She said the whole family is mystified by it. He's such a nice guy, and he treats everyone in the family with nice gifts at Christmas and for birthdays. He's very generous."

Paul eyed Connie. "The question of the evening is, are you generous?"

Connie gave Paul the slightest of smiles. She rolled down the back window of the Edsel, retrieved the portable heater from its outside post, and clipped it on the window. She rolled up the window. It was very cozy in the Edsel's roomy back seat. They didn't see much of the movie.

Paul was smitten. Connie was beautiful, intelligent, charming, and fun. He wanted to simplify his life, but she was so lovely that he wanted to see her again. He asked Connie if she would come to his next home game against the University of Vermont Catamounts. Then they would go out afterward.

CHAPTER 12

Castle College played the University of Vermont twice that year. The facilities on each campus were not very good for spectators, so both games were played at Burlington Memorial Auditorium. The rivalry between those two institutions had been fierce for many years, and Calzoni wanted to win both games badly.

Vermont was a Division 1 school, and it had played against better competition in the Yankee Conference. They had a very good team, including the all-American Bennie Berton. Berton was a black player. He was a high jumper at six feet, nine inches, and he could hit the jump shot from in close or far out. He was always a problem for Castle College.

Black players were rare in college basketball, but they were emerging in the college sport. Even though they were rare (Castle College had no black players), the ones who played were terrific.

Bill Russell and K. C. Jones led San Francisco University to a national championship and an undefeated season. Wilt Chamberlain led Kansas to a national title game. He was averaging over fifty points per game as a rookie in the NBA. Oscar Robinson once outscored an entire college team. In 1958 his team from Cincinnati defeated Seton Hall 118-54. Robertson scored fifty-six points, thus outscoring the entire opposing team.

People in the Burlington metropolitan area were highly anticipating the game, and the hype was growing in the newspapers, on the radio, and on television. George Calzoni was in his office talking over strategy for the game with Joe Mackey. "How are we going to stop Berton? He scored thirty and got twenty rebounds against us last year."

"I was thinking that maybe we could use Hayes Aldridge and Johnny White in a double pivot. They could go high-low on offense. Maybe that'll tire Berton out. On defense, we could use a 1-2-2 zone and make sure we block out on rebounds," offered Mackey.

"White is really coming along. He's been great in recent games, and he's hard to stop in practice, but I want to start our usual guys. Beemer and Aldridge are tough on the boards, but maybe, we can insert White every few minutes and see if we can frustrate Berton. The game is the day after tomorrow, so let's try out these ideas in practice today and tomorrow. I really want to win this game. We've been playing so well lately. We're on a roll. If we get in the post season tournament and keep winning, maybe we can get to Evansville for the championship game. That would be great for the school and the entire Burlington area," said Calzoni.

Calzoni worked his team hard in practice. He emphasized the importance of the game. His players responded with extra-special spirit, cooperation, and hustle. The coaches employed the double-pivot idea in practice, and it worked flawlessly. Whether or not it would work in the game was another matter. Practice concluded with some foul shots and wind sprints. They were ready for the game.

Frank Balboni had a routine every Friday night. He and his roommate would splurge for an Italian dinner at Bove's restaurant in Burlington. They would arrive at 7:30 p.m. and have a complete meal: an appetizer (calamari), dinner (veal parmesan), and dessert (cannoli). It never varied.

Remy Calvet parked his 1948 Nash down the street from Bove's. It was 8:15 p.m., and he was waiting for his accomplice to appear. He was wearing a balaclava, which covered his face except for his eyes. He was there to hurt Frank Balboni so that he wouldn't be able to play in the game against UVM. His boss had instructed him and his accomplice to jump Balboni and his roommate from behind, tackle them, and beat them around the face and body with a police baton. His boss didn't want any permanent damage but just enough so that Balboni would miss the game.

He was also instructed to take Balboni's wallet so that it would look like a mugging and a robbery. He, his accomplice, and his boss had even rehearsed the mugging and had choreographed the entire scenario. They were both getting $200 for the job, so they wanted to get it right.

He opened the door for his accomplice. They waited for Balboni and his roommate to emerge from the restaurant.

It was the night before the game against UVM. At nine o'clock in the evening, the phone rang. Calzoni's wife, Betty, answered the phone. "George, there's a detective from Burlington on the phone."

What is this about? mused Calzoni.

"Hello. Is this Coach Calzoni?"

"Yes."

"This is detective Pete Christos of the Burlington Police Department. One of your player's and his roommate were mugged and robbed after having dinner at Bove's."

"What? Mugged in Burlington? This is outrageous. This is unheard of. This is Burlington Vermont, not Detroit," hollered Calzoni.

"They're both at Fanny Allen Hospital being examined. It doesn't look like anything serious, but they were banged up pretty good. How about if I meet you over there?"

"I'll scoot right over there now."

"What was that about, dear?" asked Betty.

"One of my ballplayers was mugged in Burlington," answered Calzoni.

"Mugged? How awful. Burlington is one of the safest cities in America. Is he
one of your better players?"

He's one of my best players, and I don't think he's going to be able to play in the game against UVM. I'm going to go to Fanny Allen to see how he is."

As Calzoni went into Fanny Allen Hospital, he was met by Detective Christos and Dr. Patel.

"I was able to question the boys in Burlington. Someone heard a commotion outside of Bove's and alerted the manager, who called the police. The boys said it happened so fast that they couldn't react. They were tackled from behind and hit, with what they thought was a baseball bat, about the head, arms, legs, and back. Two men took their wallets. They were so stunned and hurt that they just lay on the sidewalk until the police arrived. Dr. Patel examined both boys. Doctor, would you tell Coach Calzoni your prognosis?" said Christos.

"Thank you, Detective Christos. Coach, I'll give you the good news first. Neither boy has any broken bones. Now here's the bad news. There are multiple contusions on each young man. There's also much swelling about the head, arms, legs, and back. They are going to be in a lot of pain for the next several days, but they should be in good shape after that. I know you have a big game tomorrow, but I would recommend that Balboni not play. He needs a few days to fully recover," explained Patel.

Calzoni looked forlorn. "This is a shock. How common is it that people get mugged?"

"It's very uncommon, Coach, and they were both obviously targeted. Did anyone know that Balboni would be at Bove's tonight?" asked Christos.

"Only everybody on the team and everybody in his dorm. He always goes to Bove's on Friday at 7:30 p.m.," said Calzoni.

"Balboni had twenty dollars in his wallet, and his roommate had fifteen. That's not much of a night's take for two muggers."

"First Aldridge and now Balboni. It seems my best players are having issues before big games."

"Did the police question Aldridge after the incident in Maine?" asked Christos.

"No. We didn't even report anything. We just thought he had food poisoning or a food allergy."

"Well, I'm going to investigate this further and determine if anyone saw anything interesting during the mugging or can identify anything at all about the two muggers."

Dr. Patel said that the two young men would be kept in the hospital overnight for observation and be released in the morning.

"Doctor, if you don't mind, I'd like to see both young men and reassure them that everything will be taken care of. Then I'm going home. I know I shouldn't do this because of my ulcer, but I'm going to have a nice big shot of Johnny Walker Black," said Calzoni.

CHAPTER 13

The next morning, the papers reported the Balboni mugging, and citizens were appalled. People called into radio news programs and demanded that police beef up security. Mackey and Calzoni were in Calzoni's office.

"You know, Coach, this just doesn't smell right."

"What do you mean?" asked Calzoni.

"Well, right before two of our biggest games, one of our best players goes down. To me, it's too much of a coincidence."

"Well, what do you think is happening, and what can we do about it?"

"I don't know what we can do about it. I guess we should just do our jobs and see if we can win this ball game," answered Mackey.

"OK. Let's talk about the ball game. We're going to have to replace Balboni. I loved the idea of the double pivot and the two big men, but I still don't want to start the two big men together. I want White to come off the bench as a sixth man."

"How about Joe Biasi?" offered Mackie. "He's looked great in practice. He loves to run, so we can put him at the point on the 1-2-2 zone. He'll run his ass off. We can use Biasi on an intermittent press to fluster their guards. He's smart and a good shooter."

"I was thinking the same thing, Joe. We're losing fifteen-to-twenty points with Balboni out. We're going to have to find those points from someone else," said Calzoni.

"Paul Fiore takes six-to-nine shots per game. We're going to have to tell him to shoot more. He has to hit some long shots to draw the defense out so that they don't collapse down on Aldridge. Fiore has a good shooting percentage. Maybe Fiore and Biasi can make up that twenty-point difference that we're losing with Balboni out," answered Mackey.

"You know, Joe, I'm starting to feel better. I loved the idea of Aldridge and White and the double pivot. Our last practice was terrific, but we're going to have to motivate the team. There's no reason that we can't go on winning. These two guys, Fiore and Biasi, as well as the rest of the team are going to have to step up. This'll be another test for us, but I feel more confident than I did with Aldridge out in Maine. We'll give them a hell, fire, and brimstone speech before the game and get them all riled up. I want them hootin' and hollerin' when they run out on that court."

In the locker room at Burlington Memorial Auditorium, Coach Cal talked to Paul Fiore.

"Listen Paul, we've lost Balboni for the game, and we have to make up that fifteen or twenty points. You've been taking about six-to-nine shots per game and doing a great job setting up the offense, but I'd like you to look for your shot more tonight. You're going to have to hit some long bombs to draw the defense out; otherwise, they're going to collapse down on Aldridge and bottle him up. I don't mean start heaving the ball every chance you get but be smart. If you're in the clear, take the shot. When the defense comes out on you, feed the ball into Aldridge. I want you to play your regular game. You're the guard. Control the tempo, but just take a few more shots. Get it?" said Calzoni.

"Don't worry, Coach. I've got it."

While Calzoni was talking to Fiore, Mackey took Biasi aside. "Joe, you're starting tonight." Biasi could hardly control himself. He was euphoric. He had waited for this opportunity since enrolling at Castle College. "You're taking Balboni's place tonight. Coach Cal and I both think you're the best option. You will be at the point in the 1-2-2 zone, and we want you to pressure the ball when their guards bring it up court. Try to fluster them and take them out of their comfort zone. Maybe we can score a few points on turnovers. Also, don't be afraid to shoot. We have to make up those fifteen-to-twenty points that Balboni usually contributes, so keep those hands up on defense at the point on the zone and wave your arms," said Mackey.

"I'm going to run my ass off, Coach. They won't know what hit them."

It was almost time to take the court. Calzoni and Mackey made some final comments.

"Look, fellas, we've had some adversity this year, but we're really playing well now. We had some bad luck with Aldridge in Maine, but if it wasn't for that, we'd be undefeated. I truly feel that we can go all the way to the championship with this team. Let's not let UVM get in our way. We can beat them!

"Balboni wanted to be here, but I told him to rest in the dorm and listen to the game on the radio, but let's dedicate the game to Balboni. Joe Biasi is going to start in his place, and I know that Joe is going to do a great job. He's a hustler. He's going to hound those guards all over the court. I want all you guys to be mindful of Berton. When he gets the ball down low, I want you to collapse on him and try to knock the ball away. When he puts the ball on the floor, stay in his path. Let's frustrate him. I have a positive feeling. We're going to win this game! Now let's get in a circle and put our hands together. Are we gonna win?" yelled Calzoni.

Mackey joined in. His face was red, and the vein on the side of his neck was throbbing.

"Let's get out on the court and kick some ass!" yelled Mackey.

The team surged out on the court like the Running of the Bulls in Pamplona, Spain.

During the warm-ups, Jack Bonnet, who was dressed in his raccoon coat with megaphone ready, wandered over to Coach Cal. "How's Balboni, Coach? Is he out for the season?"

"No, he should be back in a few days. He just needs some rest and some time for all the bruises to heal," said Cal.

"What do you think your chances are tonight?"

"I think they're good. We made some adjustments. Joe Biasi is starting. He's been waiting for this chance. He's going to run their guards ragged. And I think you'll be pleasantly surprised with Johnny White. We're going to use him to frustrate Berton."

"All the news' outlets are favoring UVM to win with Balboni out," said Bonnet.

"Well, I have some news for you and everybody else. We're going to win."

The decibel level of the crowd was deafening. Jack Bonnet was running up and down the sidelines yelling through his megaphone and exhorting the crowd. The Castle College ROTC band was playing their fight song. The starting lineups for both teams had been announced, and the game was about to begin.

Castle College had a set play off the center court jump ball. Aldridge tipped the ball to Fiore, Tate ran a screen on Biasi's man, and Biasi sprinted to the basket for a lay-up off Fiore's pass. Biasi pressured the ball, but UVM managed to get the ball over the mid-court line. Biasi was a dynamo as he made it difficult for them to make cross-court passes by waving his arms and moving his feet at the point on the zone. As planned, Castle College collapsed on Berton whenever he received the ball. He was getting frustrated.

Fiore hit three long shots in a row and Biasi hit two. UVM had to come out to defend these two players, which freed up Aldridge to score from in close. White came in for Tate, and that made it even more difficult for Berton because he had to contend with two big men surrounding him.

Castle College's strategy was working, and the team was gaining more confidence as the game progressed. As the first half came to a close, they were ahead by eighteen points.

In the second half, UVM made a run and got the lead down to six points, but Castle College rallied, and the final score was 72-60 in favor of Castle College. Castle College's crowd was ecstatic as they stormed the court and lifted the starting five on their shoulders and escorted them to the locker room.

George Calzone and Joe Mackey were all smiles in the locker room as they made the rounds congratulating all the players. Calzoni was especially proud of Biasi. "Joe, you really made a difference tonight. You and Johnny White are giving me and Coach Mackey a good problem. You and White are playing so well that you are earning more playing time. You know that I always like to play five guys for most of the game, but we're evolving. Now I can insert either you or White into the game and get quality minutes. It's a wonderful problem to have as a coach. Keep working hard and be ready if you're called upon because you're definitely going to get more minutes when Balboni returns. Fantastic job!" Calzoni said as he patted Biasi on the back.

"You don't have to worry about me, Coach. I'm always ready. I want to play," said Biasi.

CHAPTER 14

After the game, Barry Gleason, Corrine, Connie, and Paul all hopped into Barry's Edsel and went for some Chinese food. They were all in a celebratory mood, especially Paul. As they ate they talked about the game.

"Joe Biasi proved to be a capable replacement for Balboni," said Barry.

"Joe's been waiting for this opportunity for a long time. He works hard in practice, and he's smart. When the coach tells Joe to do something, he's not only able to execute the play but also able to see the options. He's able to adapt if another opportunity presents itself. That's smart basketball. A lot of players with more ability do not have that talent. So now when Joe comes in to substitute, his teammates have confidence in him.

"It was terrible what happened to Balboni, but in a way, his misfortune is making us stronger. The players on our team are feeling more and more confident. We're going to be very tough to beat," said Paul.

"When was the last time Castle College won a championship?" asked Connie.

"I don't think they've ever won a championship," said Paul.

"What about the two incidents that happened to Aldridge and Balboni?" asked Corrine.

"Listen. Like I said, it's terrible what happened to them, but it's made us stronger and more resilient. The players on the team are also looking out for each other and being careful. If anything seems out of whack, we've all agreed to report it immediately to the coach. We don't want any more incidents," said Paul.

"Do you think there is any subterfuge going on? Do you think the two incidents are connected in any way?" asked Connie.

"I've had discussions with some of the players about Aldridge's disappearance and Balboni's mugging. We don't think there is any connection, but we're going to try to be more observant and look out for each other." said Paul. The discussion turned to that night's victory as they consumed their dinners.

Remy Calvet pulled up to his house in Colchester, Vermont. The door to his 1948 Nash squeaked as he opened it. Before ascending the outside steps to his second-floor apartment, he retrieved some WD-40 from the trunk to squirt on the hinges of the Nash's front door. Even though the car was old, he loved it. He wanted to make sure that it was in fine working condition.

Remy limped up the steps and unlocked the door to his apartment. His limp was courtesy of an injury that had occurred at basketball practice many years earlier. He was dressed in a denim shirt, jeans, and work boots, which were covered in dirt and dust. He was a handyman, and he had spent the day repairing brick and concrete steps.

He had advertised his skills in the town's paper. He was well versed in carpentry, masonry, roofing, and plumbing. Although he was not an expert in any of these professions, he had developed a reputation as a trusted handyman. When there was an emergency, people called him. He had had many repeat customers.

Remy's apartment was dingy and sparse. It had four rooms: a kitchen, living room, bedroom, and bathroom. Most of the furniture had been donated by friends and acquaintances.

Remy liked to go out the night before garbage pickup. He would ride around Colchester, Winooski, and Burlington and throw furniture or other items that looked good into his trunk. He had refinished many pieces of furniture and outfitted his apartment with these items.

Remy was thirty-five years old. His hair was thinning and a reddish-blond color. He had brown eyes, thin lips, a pointy chin, and a long thin neck. His chin sported a goatee that needed to be trimmed. He was not married, and his social life was dominated by drinking at seedy bars. These bars were outside of the area of where he worked because he did not want to alienate any of his clientele.

Remy was exhausted from work. He took off his work boots and shirt. He opened the refrigerator door and took out a tall, cold can of beer. He popped the tab, tilted the beer to his lips, and drank the whole can in one hardy chug. Then he heard the phone ring in the kitchen and got up to answer it.

"Remy, it's the boss. I want to thank you again for the great job that you did with Balboni."

"Thanks, boss. When do I get my money?"

"I have it for you right here—ten twenties in cash. I made a shitload of money on the game, and I'm very happy. Our inside guy alerted me to the changes Castle College was making during practice. The point spread and odds of the game changed. UVM was expected to win because Balboni was out, but with the changes Castle College was making, I figured that Castle College had the better chance of winning. I bet all my money on them and came out of it with a tidy sum," said the boss.

"Do you want me to do anything else for you?" asked Calvet.

"No, I'm happy with the outcome. Let's lie low for a while. I'm getting my cues from the higher-ups in Boston, and they want to wait for another big game. That's where all the action is."

"OK, boss. Call me when you need me," said Calvet.

Remy Calvet loved doing these side jobs. He had long hated anything that had to do with basketball, and he felt justified in doing anything that would hurt the sport. The fact that all of the incidents involved Castle College was irrelevant. It didn't matter who the team was. His feelings against the game were insatiable. The game had given him nothing but misery. It stemmed from an incident where he had broken his leg during basketball practice. This had left him with a lifelong limp. The ridicule that he had received from his peers had been demoralizing. It had shaped him into a pessimistic and mean individual. Whatever the future jobs were, he would do them willingly.

⊹≈≈⊱ ⊰≈≈⊹

Midterm exams were scheduled to start soon, and Paul Fiore was barely earning Cs in his business courses, even though he was being tutored. Connie Barbeau had mentioned to Paul that her father was a CPA, so she was very familiar with business terminology. She offered to help him if he could get to Champlain College's library. The library had a place where students could meet and study. Barry Gleason was very generous with his car. He and Paul would tale dates out, go out to eat, and do errands, using the car, so Barry offered to drive Paul to Champlain College whenever he wanted to study with Connie.

Paul was not a slacker. He diligently studied his business assignments. With the tutoring and Connie's help, he was starting to understand the concepts of his courses. He hoped to raise his grades into the B range. Now that seemed like a distinct possibility.

Earlier in the year, he had felt under a great deal of pressure because of his poor grades and the situation with his girlfriend back in New Jersey. That was all changing. He had received help with his courses on multiple fronts, Connie was lovely, and his team was on a winning streak. He was indeed very confident about the future.

CHAPTER 15

Castle College continued to win without further incident. Their record ballooned to 24-1, and they were atop the Northeast Conference. The team had evolved from the beginning of the year. In the past, Calzoni had kept a script of his starting five playing the entire game, but now he was substituting Johnny White and Joe Biasi freely. Johnny White relieved Hayes Aldridge, making a rested Aldridge more effective. Coach Calzoni also used them together, employing the double pivot.

With Aldridge's tutelage, White had improved his shooting, blocking out, rebounding, and passing. White had developed a sweeping hook shot to go along with his jump shot. He was learning to shoot with his left hand as well as his right from in close. Castle College was one of the few teams in the country that had two seven-footers who could play effectively at the same time.

Over the course of the season, the team had reached a level of comfort and consistency. All members of the team had improved their games. Fiore, Balboni, Beemer, and Tate had all improved their shooting percentage as well as other areas of the game like assists and rebounding. On defense, they adapted to the rival team's players, although they usually opted for a man-to-man defense. If they were playing zone, Biasi would run havoc at the point on the 1-2-2 zone.

They had learned how to win. What made a winning team? A winning team was a smart team. It was a team that knew how to exploit the weaknesses of its opponent at the end of the game: blocking out on rebounds, keeping hands up on defense to knock the ball away, positioning oneself to take a charge, hitting the open man, and being confident to hit the open shot at the end of the game. It was the team that utilized the fundamentals of the game to win. That was Castle College.

In their last two games, Castle College had defeated two very good teams in their conference: Merrimack and Assumption. In a week, they would be playing for the championship of their conference against their nemesis, Saint Anselm. If they beat Saint Anselm, they would qualify for the National Division II NCAA Tournament. Saint Anselm was the only team that had defeated Castle College, but the team had been without Hayes Aldridge, so the team was chomping at the bit for revenge.

Several days before the big game, Detective Pete Christos walked into Calzoni's office.

"Coach, I want to make you aware of an investigation into the manipulation of point spreads in college basketball games. I received a call from the FBI office in Boston. Apparently, they're investigating a syndicate that is involved in these activities all over New England. Their tentacles are spread into Maine, New Hampshire, Vermont, Massachusetts, Rhode Island, and Connecticut. They have been investigating anomalies that have been occurring at a myriad of colleges."

"What do you mean by anomalies?" asked Calzoni.

"Well, incidents like what happened to your two players: players getting hurt under mysterious circumstances, players not showing up for games, and players receiving threats—things that are happening and aren't normal. They are anomalies."

"What do you want me to do, Detective? I'll cooperate with you 100 percent."

"I want you to be alert to anything that occurs beyond the norm. It could be a change in a player's behavior or anybody outside of the team that is interfering in some way with your program. Be alert to the most minute detail. Keep your eyes and ears open and don't be afraid to contact me at any time and even if the incident seems trivial. Sometimes the smallest detail can blow a case wide open," said Christos.

"I'll inform Joe Mackey of the investigation and instruct him to also be observant."

"I'd like to also question Aldridge. He may be part of it."

"No way, Detective. He doesn't need any money. He lives in Franklin Lakes, New Jersey, a very upscale community. He attended Bergen Catholic, a very highly rated high school. His mother is a physician, and his father works in advertising in New York. It doesn't make any sense that he would be involved," said Calzoni.

"There are a lot of questions that I have for him about what happened in Maine. He had some tea after the pregame meal. He went for a walk, sat down on a park bench, and then he blacked out. It has lots of holes in it. It doesn't hold water."

"You're welcome to question Aldridge. That's your job, but I just don't see it."

"I'd also like to informally question your other players just to see if I can detect anything untoward."

"Like I said, you're welcome to question anyone at any time. If anything is going on, I'd like to know about it. One caveat detective. Could you wait until after our game with Saint Anselm? I want our team to be focused, and I don't want any distractions. I would really appreciate that," said Calzoni.

"I understand, Coach. I'll wait until after the game."

"The game is being played at Boston Garden a week from today, and buses are being rented so a contingent of students can ride down. We want a big student section to make a lot of noise and support our players. We're going to be outnumbered by Saint Anselm's fans because Manchester, New Hampshire, is closer to Boston than we are. It's going to be a big event for our players, our students, and the entire Burlington area, so I thank you again," said Calzoni.

CHAPTER 16

Remy Calvet received a call from his boss.

"Listen Remy. I've been alerted from the higher-ups in Boston that the players on the Castle College team are going to be questioned by Detective Christos. There's a wide-ranging investigation going on about point fixing and point spreads in college basketball. I'm concerned that our inside guy might crack under questioning. If he cracks, we're going to jail for a long time. The higher-ups want me to take care of it. If I don't, they're going to take care of me and you. Do you understand?" said the boss.

"What do you mean take care of it?" asked Calvet.

"We have to get rid of him."

"What?" said Remy. "Count me out!"

"What choice do we have? I told you that if we don't take care of it, they'll take care of us. The syndicate is betting a lot of money on Saint Anselm to win. They think Castle College will be in a funk if a player is killed. It'll take their minds off the game. The syndicate thinks this is good business," said the boss. "I have a plan that I think will work and cannot be traced. Call our inside guy at his dorm and tell him that I want to meet him down the street from the campus at 10:00 p.m. in the Stewart's parking lot. It should take about twenty minutes to walk there. He should be walking on the shoulder of the road, so at 9:50 p.m., I want you to speed down the road and run him over."

"You want me to kill him?" Remy was incredulous.

"Like I told you, what choice do we have?"

"You want me to use my car? I love that car. It's going to get all dented up."

"Your car is a piece of shit. Who else in Vermont has a 1948 Nash Rambler? Do they even make that car anymore? It's all dented up anyway. Here's the deal. I'll pay you $500 for the job, and I'll repair any damage done to the car. I'll even throw in a new paint job," said the boss.

Remy hesitated a few seconds to think it over. "I guess we're in a bind, and this is the only way out. OK, I'll do it."

"I'm glad that you see it my way. Let's get this done as soon as possible. Call him tonight," said the boss.

Remy's inside man and accomplice was called at his college dorm. The snack bar on campus was closed, and he and his roommate were always hungry. He left with an order for two root beers and two hot dogs for himself and his roommate and headed off to Stewart's. He left at 9:40 p.m. to meet his boss in the Stewart's parking lot.

He was walking along the shoulder of the road at 9:50 p.m., when he heard the familiar clanging and clattering of tire chains. The clattering was getting louder as a car approached him at high speed. As he looked around, he was mesmerized by the headlights' blinding orbs. The car clipped him on his left side, hurtling him high off the ground as his arms and legs twirled and he went head over heels like a rag doll flying through the air. He landed ten feet away on his back in a snowbank on the side of the road as the car sped away. As he lay there in an unmoving clump, blood spurted from his mouth and seeped out of his ears and nose. Nat Parro gazed up at the stars with unseeing eyes.

Remy Calvet was ecstatic. For years he had had a vendetta against basketball. After all those years of limping and people making fun of him, he finally felt vindicated. He was glad that he had run down Nat Parro. Parro was a clown, and he didn't even like the guy. He finally had gotten his revenge. He had made $500 on the deal, and he was going to celebrate. He was going to have his car repaired and repainted. He was going to go to the best restaurant that he could find in Burlington and have a gourmet meal.

He didn't think anyone had seen him run down Parro. It was dark out, and no one seemed to be at Stewart's, so he thought he was in the clear. He turned on his car radio to his favorite rock-and-roll station and hummed as he sailed on home.

The team was devastated when they heard the news of Parro's demise. Coaches Calzoni, Mackey, and the players all agreed that the best honor that they could bestow on Parro was to attend Mass, which was held at the college chapel, and pray for his soul, even though members of the team were of different denominations.

Parro would be missed. He was not someone who received much playing time during games, but he worked hard in practice and kept everyone loose in the locker room with his joking, antics, and pranks. The team did not know, however, that he had received money for his participation in Balboni's mugging or that he had aided in Aldridge's blackout in Maine. The players decided to have a team meeting at the Castle College Student Center.

"Look, guys, I know this was a devastating loss, but we have the championship game coming up against Saint Anselm. If we beat them, we'll go to the Division II National Tournament in Evansville, Indiana. We have to focus. I don't know about you guys, but I want to go to Evansville. We can't let anything deter us," said Fiore.

"This is a chance of a lifetime, and I'm a senior. I'll never get this chance again" said Aldridge.

"We took care of Merrimack and Assumption easily. Let's kick the shit out of Saint Anselm. They're the only team that beat us this year," said Balboni.

"Let's honor Parro by going all the way. Agreed?" said Beemer.

"Let's do it!" everybody joined in.

A day after the tragic hit-and-run of Nat Parro, Detective Christos called Coach Calzoni. "Coach, we caught a break on the hit-and-run. A man at Stewart's saw a car speed away and gave us sort of a description of the car. The car was dark blue, but he had trouble identifying the make of the car. It wasn't one of the big three automobiles like Chrysler, General Motors, or Ford. It was an off-brand like a Kaiser Fraser, Studebaker, or Nash. He wasn't sure, but at least we have something to work on. I'm going to do a blitz of all the auto-body shops in the area. It was dented up pretty good, so if the car is being repaired, maybe we'll get lucky and be able to identify the owner."

"That's great news, Detective. Keep me posted on what happens," said Calzoni.

Several days after Detective Christos's call, Coach Calzoni could detect the pleasant aroma of apple-scented pipe smoke emanating from his outer office. Calzoni's secretary knocked on his door and entered.

"Mr. Calzoni, Detective Christos is here to see you. Are you available? He says it's very important."

"Of course. Send him in," said Calzoni.

Detective Christos entered, puffing on his pipe. "May I take a seat, Coach?" asked Christos.

"Make yourself comfortable. What's up?"

"I wanted to meet with you in person to tell you the news. You won't believe this, Coach, but we've broken the case wide open."

"That's fantastic news. You're right, I don't believe it," said Calzoni.

"We did a sweep of all auto-body shops in the area, and Hal's Body Shop in Colchester had a 1948 dark-blue Nash Rambler in for repairs and a paint job. The owner of the car is this numbskull named Remy Calvet, who lives in Colchester. You would think that someone who committed a hit-and-run crime would try to go as far away as possible to repair his car, but no, he went to the closest auto-body shop to his house. When we questioned him, he started babbling and telling us everything. He gave up his boss, who is Harry Casey. It was incredible."

"Harry Casey is his boss? You mean the barber on Church Street?" asked Calzoni.

"Right. Casey had been running some small book out of his barbershop for many years. He caught wind of a syndicate down in Boston and realized that he could make some big money. Here's the part that you are going to be shocked about and won't like. Casey recruited Nat Parro as an accomplice to Remy Calvet. Parro assisted him in Maine and also with the mugging of Balboni," said Christos.

"Nat Parro was involved in this? I don't believe it."

"Sorry to say, Coach, but it's true. Let me tell you what we found out from Calvet's interrogation. When Casey hooked up with the syndicate, he needed someone to help him out, so he recruited Calvet. Calvet was a roofer and a handyman, who was always looking for extra money. Calvet had a vendetta against basketball, which stemmed from an incident that happened in high school. He had been trying out for the team, and he had broken his hip and leg going up for a rebound, which resulted in a limp for the rest of his life.

"His peers made fun of him and called him gimp. He also had an issue with the high school coach, who would not let him be team manager after his injury. Calvet was ripe for revenge in any form against the sport.

"When Parro came in for his haircuts, he was always complaining about not having enough money. When Parro found out that Casey was a bookie, he started betting big-time. He bet on everything: hockey, basketball, horse racing, you name it, and he started losing. Parro got into such a deep hole that he didn't know how he was going to pay it back. Parro had a gambling problem that he could not control.

"Casey came up with a plan: Parro could work off the debt by being an informant. Parro would be invaluable as an inside man. He could tell Casey about any strategies that the team was planning that might affect the outcome of games and any other useful information. Casey also used this information in communications with the syndicate in Boston. The syndicate used the information to set and manipulate point spreads and betting lines.

"When your team was in Maine, Casey devised a plan to take Aldridge out of the game. Parro had informed Casey of Aldridge's habit of having herbal tea before an away game so that he could relax. Calvet drove to Maine with a sedative that Casey had obtained from a dentist friend. The sedative would take some time to work, but they made sure that they gave him a double dose. It would make him woozy and then put him to sleep for a couple of hours, which is what happened.

"Calvet and Parro made sure they were close to Aldridge's room when the tea was being delivered to there. When room service appeared, Parro distracted the waiter, and Calvet spiked the tea with the sedative. The syndicate back in Boston knew of this collusion and changed the betting lines for the game. They made a ton of money as a result.

"With Balboni, Parro informed Casey of Balboni's habit of going to Bove's every Friday night at 7:30 p.m., so that Parro and Calvet could pull off the mugging."

"What about the hit-and-run?" asked Calzoni.

"Casey was afraid that Parro would crack under questioning. He had Calvet lure Parro to Stewart's so that Parro could meet with the boss, and that's when Calvet ran him down. It was a stupid and unnecessary thing to do," said Christos.

"So obviously, you don't need to question anyone on the team."

"No, I don't. You can go into your championship game with a clear conscience. By the way, the syndicate in Boston has been busted by the FBI, so you don't have to worry about its nonsense. Go into the game with a clear head and purpose and bring home a championship to Castleport, Vermont. Then I hope you can go all the way for the national championship in Evansville," said Christos.

"Me too," said Calzoni. "Thanks for your fine work!"

CHAPTER 17

That same day after practice, Calzoni called a team meeting and repeated the scenario that Detective Christos had described. The players were quiet during the whole explanation and horrified that one of their teammates had acted as an informer and an accomplice.

"I can't believe that Parro was such a turncoat. He didn't deserve to die, but why was he so damn greedy? What did he make—a few hundred dollars? He put himself and the team in jeopardy. Who knows what else would have happened if this wasn't put to rest. This is a shock, but I'm glad it's over," said Joe Biasi.

"The detective also said that the syndicate in Boston that was running the scam has been busted. We don't have to worry about any more monkey business. The only thing we have to worry about is winning the basketball game against Saint Anselm, and if we're lucky, we're going to Evansville," said Calzoni.

"You know, when I heard your story, Coach, I thought you were going to say that Jack Bonnet was behind all this and not Harry Casey," said Fiore.

"Why would you think that Bonnet was behind it?" asked Calzoni.

"Well, he has this big car, a big house, and a lot of money. He's only a manager at Sears, so I thought he might be behind this scam."

"I don't know where Bonnet gets his money, but he has been a loyal fan and contributor to our program for many years. It would be incomprehensible to me that he would run a scam involving Castle College," said Calzoni.

"That's the story men. Get showered and rested. We'll have one more practice tomorrow, and then the day after that, we go to Boston to play Saint Anselm. If we get by them, we're in the national spotlight."

Burlington Free Press interviewed Detective Pete Christos and ran an in-depth feature article about the Nat Parro murder and the incidents leading up to it. The paper recounted the mugging of Balboni and the drugging of Aldridge in Maine. The article resulted in a multitude of letters to the editor, as well as a renewed interest in Castle College's team.

The team would be staying at the Loews Boston Hotel. Usually trips to Boston were a one-day affair because it was only a four-hour drive from Burlington, but Calzoni wanted the team to rest. He would hold a light shoot around and practice before dinner, but he wanted all players in their rooms by 9:00 p.m. The next day, it would be breakfast, a team meeting going over strategy, the pregame meet, and then the game would be played at 3:00 p.m.

The night before the team left for Boston, Barry Gleason, Paul, Connie, and Corrine went to The Mill. As usual, Jack Bonnet was holding court and drinking some beers. Jack had heard about the scenario with Parro and Casey through the grapevine and had also read the feature article in the *Burlington Free Press*. He wanted to commiserate with Paul and offer encouragement for the upcoming game.

"I read about what happened with Aldridge, Balboni, and Parro. What an incredible series of events. Now you guys can concentrate on the game," said Bonnet.

"You know, when I was listening to Calzoni's description of what happened, I hope you won't be insulted, but I thought you were behind the scam," said Fiore.

"Me? You have a big set of balls to say that. I am insulted. How could you think that I was behind it?"

"You have that gorgeous Cadillac de Ville, you live in a mansion, and you're very generous with your money. How can you afford all that on your salary as a manager at Sears?" asked Fiore.

"It isn't any of your business where I get my money, but I'll tell you anyway. I've been investing in stocks for many years, and I'm very good at it. I have stock in AT&T, IBM, General Motors, and many other companies. I have quite a comprehensive portfolio. When the stocks are low, I buy, and when they're high, I sell. I've made a lot of money over the years. Perhaps if Harry Casey had learned to invest instead of being a bookie, Nat Parro would still be alive, and Harry would still be giving haircuts in his barbershop," said Bonnet.

"Okay, I apologize. But can you see how I would think that you were behind it."

"There is no way that I would do anything to hurt this team. It's a big part of my life. Every year, I can't wait for basketball season to start, and I've contributed to and supported the team with time and money over the years. I will continue to do that, and I will be in Boston with my megaphone and raccoon coat. If you get to Evansville, I'll be there too," said Bonnet.

"Now good luck to you in the coming game. Don't stay out too late. I want you to be in good shape for the game."

The capacity of the seating in Boston Garden was almost twenty thousand, but for college games, the Garden would curtain off the top tier of the stands because a college game usually drew fewer people than a professional hockey or basketball game. If a college game drew eight thousand fans, it would seem like a capacity crowd. The stands were packed with students, alumni, and college basketball fans. The game was being broadcast on radio and television back to Burlington.

Castle College was pumped about the game. They were confident because they would have a full contingent this time, including Aldridge for the game. The players took the court and got ready for the center jump, where Aldridge had a decided height advantage.

If a team could score off a center jump, it gave them a little bit of momentum to start the game.

The referee tossed the ball and Aldridge tapped it long toward Castle College's basket, where Beemer retrieved it and scored the first basket. Everything was going according to plan. Aldridge was scoring. Fiore and Balboni were scoring from long range, and Beemer and Tate were rebounding and throwing the ball up court so that the guards could start the fast break. Castle College was ahead by fifteen points midway through the first half, when Aldridge caught an elbow to the chin, which opened up a big gash. Blood spurted from the injury, and he had to be taken out of the game.

Calzoni looked over at Dr. Jim Bombard. "Jim. Do you know how to stitch? You've got to help me out here, pal. If Aldridge doesn't play, we don't win. You've got to do me this one big favor. Can you do that for me? The season is riding on it. Are you OK?"

"I know how to stitch, Coach, and I'm fine. I drink after the game, not before it," said Bombard.

"If you patch him up, I'll buy you a whole gallon of Chevas Regal. Now get him to the locker room and sew him up so I can get him back in the game."

"He'll be back before you know it," said Bombard.

Fans could see confidence building in the demeanor of the Saint Anselm players. They thought it would be the same outcome as what had happened in Maine, but Calzoni substituted Johnny White for Aldridge, and White went to work. He was now in the spotlight, and he did not disappoint. White was a totally different player that he had been in the first game because he had benefitted from Aldridge's tutelage.

White immediately scored on two sweeping hook shots, a tap in, and a jump shot from the corner. The confidence that Saint Anselm had gained with Aldridge's injury quickly deflated as Castle College maintained its lead into the half-time break. As the first half ended, fans were becoming concerned because Aldridge had not returned.

As Castle College went into the locker room at halftime, Dr.

Bombard was finishing up his masterpiece. Hayes Aldridge's gash was appropriately stitched, and it was being covered by a gauze pad, so he was ready to go in the second half. Calzoni went over to Bombard and gave him a big hug as the rest of the team cheered.

With Aldridge back in the second half, Saint Anselm had no chance. Everything was working for Castle College: the press, the1-2-2 zone, the double pivot, and the long bombs of Balboni and Fiore. It was a clinic on how the game was meant to be played. Castle College won by twenty-five points. They were going to Evansville!

CHAPTER 18

The players were excited about playing in Indiana. In the 1950s and 1960s, Indiana was the mecca of high school and college basketball. The people were such fanatics that they would shut down entire towns so that the populace could attend the high school or college basketball game. It was such a hotbed for the sport that everything took a back seat to it. High school stars were instant celebrities and revered in their towns. The sport was played all year round in schoolyards, and rivalries were intense.

The team boarded the plane for their flight to Evansville. Many of the players had never flown before, so there was a bit of trepidation about the flight. The entourage included the two coaches, their families, ten players, Mike Tragussi (the team's manager), Dr. Jim Bombard (the team's doctor), TV and radio crews from WCAX in Burlington, and their announcer, Tony Adams, who would be doing a simulcast of the game back to Burlington, Vermont.

Jack Bonnet had also subsidized his own entourage, which included important townspeople as well as Barry Gleason, his girlfriend Corrine, and Connie Barbeau. As Jack had stated to Paul Fiore at The Mill, he had been the team's top fan and historian for over twenty years, and he was not going to miss this momentous occasion.

The plane took off, and the flight was relatively uneventful until they were about fifteen minutes away from Evansville. At that point, the pilot said over the loudspeaker that passengers should fasten their seat belts. "We are encountering some turbulence. There are thunderstorms and tornadoes in the area. All seat belts must be worn until further notice," said the captain.

The plane began to wobble, as if it were a car riding at high speed over an unpaved road with potholes. The plane swayed up and down and back and forth. The plane dropped forty feet and then rose again. It was out of control, and it continued to wobble. Books and magazines flew around the cabin as passengers screamed and hugged each other out of fear.

The captain came on the loudspeaker again. "We're flying into an unexpected one-hundred-mile-per-hour headwind. It should only last for several more minutes, but we're going to try to land." This announcement elicited even more screams and horror from the passengers as the plane continued to shudder.

Several minutes later the captain spoke again. "Make sure that all seat belts are fastened. We are preparing to land." The plane continued to jounce as it descended down, down, and somehow, it touched down safely as the passengers hooted for joy as they gave the pilots a sitting ovation. The players were shaken and in a state of shock. What a welcome to Evansville that was.

Castle College would participate in the Division II National Championship Final Four Tournament at the Ford Center in Evansville, Indiana. They would be staying at a nearby Holiday Inn.

Philadelphia Textile would play Evansville, and Castle College would play Belmont Abbey. The winners of those two games would play each other for the championship.

Castle College's first opponent would be Belmont Abbey. They were a very good team, but the spotlight would be on their coach, Al McGuire. Al McGuire had been a player for the New York Knickerbockers, from 1951–1955, along with his brother, Dick McGuire. Dick McGuire was the better player, but Al was the better coach. Al McGuire never averaged more than six points per game for the Knicks. He was known more for his showmanship than he was for his playing ability. Whenever the Knicks played the Celtics, McGuire would say,

"I want Cousy. I'm going to stop him. I'm going to embarrass him!" The newspapers picked this up and made it a headline in their sports' pages. The papers enjoyed his braggadocio because it made good copy for them, and the front office liked it because it put fans in the stands.

McGuire, however, made his mark as a coach. He was a great coach with a decided flair for the dramatic. At Belmont Abbey games, he would let his assistant coach take care of all the pregame preliminaries while McGuire was nowhere to be seen. His players worried about him and asked where he was or if he was OK.

McGuire strode in several minutes before the game started. His black hair was neatly coiffed, and he was dressed impeccably in a dark-blue suit, a red tie, and shoes that were so polished to a blinding sheen that he immediately psyched up his players. During the game, he encouraged and yelled at his players, baited the refs, and strode up and down the sidelines. He was the whole show.

Castle College had no trouble with Belmont Abbey. The only trouble that they had during the game was with their own assistant coach, Joe Mackey. Calzoni said to Mackey during the game, "Joe, get your head in the game. Stop watching McGuire." Evansville defeated Philadelphia Textile, so the championship game would be between Castle College and Evansville.

CHAPTER 19

Evansville was the defending national champion. They had won the Division II tournament in 1959. They had consistently been a top team over the years.

Jerry Stone, their all-American, top player, was six feet, seven inches tall, and he could play guard or forward. If they wanted to win the game, they had to stop him. Stone was Fiore and Balboni's responsibility. The strategy was to use a modified box where Fiore or Balboni would follow Stone all over the court while the rest of the team played zone against the other players. Stone was known for his perpetual motion while he didn't have the ball to free himself up for shots. It would be a difficult assignment for Fiore or Balboni.

In the locker room before the championship game, Calzoni gave his special pregame talk to the team. "Here we are guys. I've never coached a team that was beset with so many difficulties and tragedies or was so fantastically gifted, but here we are. You never gave up, and instead of folding, you just got better. If anyone ever deserved to win the national championship, it's you guys, but nobody is going to give it to you. You have to earn it. Let's do that today. Let's earn it. Let's take it.

"You've learned all kinds of offenses and defenses this year. You know all the drills, so if I ask you to do something during the game, do it, and if you have any questions, don't be afraid to ask. This game is too important.

"We're going to start out with a box on Stone, but during the game, we might have to adapt to something else. We'll see how it goes. Stone is our biggest threat, so just like Berton from UVM, I want you to collapse on Stone whenever possible. Fiore is going to guard Stone, so whenever Stone gets the ball, annoy him. Try to slap the ball away.

"Stone likes to go to his right, so Fiore is going to overplay him and try to make him go to his left. If our zone is not working and Stone's teammates start to hit the outside shot, we might have to go to a straight-up, man-to-man defense.

"Remember, I've told you a million times, fundamentals win games. Block out and keep your hands up on defense. After a rebound, get the ball up court to one of the guards so we can start the fast break. We're going to start out with a modified press to see how their guards handle it, but I want you to pick up the guards at mid-court regardless.

"Hustle. Get in their faces. Dive for loose balls. Play your heart out. This is a chance that only a few special teams ever get. Let's make it special so that everyone who is here, is listening, or watching will never forget it! Now let's all gather round and put our hands together, and let's go out and win this championship!" The players yelled in unison and stormed onto the court.

Tyler Jones was Evansville's big man, but he was no match for Hayes Aldridge. Castle College had the edge in the pivot with Aldridge and Johnny White. Dan Mumford and Tommy Lord were both forwards, and Jay Styles was the playmaking guard, but the big problem was Jerry Stone, who was very difficult to guard. Calzoni and Mackey had their strategy set for the game, but they would have to adapt as needed and as the game evolved.

Ten thousand fans were on their feet clapping and cheering as the game began. Aldridge tapped the ball to Tate off the center jump, but Stone knocked it away to Styles, who passed it to Mumford for a score.

Evansville put on a full-court press as Castle College inbounded the ball. Castle College was able to get the ball into the front court with little difficulty. They threw the ball into the corner where Aldridge drilled a jump shot. When Evansville threw the ball in bounds, Castle College went into their press. It seemed that both teams had similar strategies.

Fiore guarded Stone all over the court while the rest of the team played zone. Fiore hounded him. Fiore's teammates helped out and collapsed on Stone whenever he got the ball.

This strategy made the zone vulnerable, as Styles, Lord, and Mumford proved to be deadly shooters. When Castle College collapsed on Stone, Styles, Lord, and Mumford had open shots that they converted.

Evansville was ahead by eight points with five minutes left in the first half when Calzoni called for a time-out. "Listen, guys, we're going to have to go to a man-to-man defense. No more box and one on Stone. It isn't working. Fiore, I want you to stay on Stone. I want the rest of you to continue to collapse on him but to also guard those other guys. They're good shooters. Joe, could you take over."

"Hayes, you take Tyler Jones. Luke, you're on Mumford. Frank, take Styles. Wally, you take Lord. Paul, stay on Stone. Remember to keep your hands up on defense and overplay these guys to their weak sides if possible. These guys are good, but we're better. Keep hustling," said Mackey.

The man-to-man defense proved to be the better option, but Castle College was still down by three points as they headed into the half-time break. Calzoni urged the team to continue with the man-to-man defense and reviewed the strengths and weaknesses of their opponents as they prepared for the final half of the game.

During the second half, Stone continued his perpetual motion, getting free for shots and feeding his teammates. The game continued to go back and forth.

Hayes Aldridge and Johnny White were working well together. Castle College's score went up by five points, but Evansville rallied and tied the score. The noise in the arena was deafening, and the fans were thrilled by this evenly matched and entertaining game.

With ten seconds to go, Castle College was up by one point, but Stone freed himself up in the corner and drained a jump shot. Castle College got the ball up over the mid-court line and called a time-out with five seconds to go. Evansville was up by one point as Castle College's team went over a set play that they had rehearsed for this type of situation. Calzoni substituted Johnny White for Luke Tate.

Everyone expected Aldridge to get the ball, but Balboni inbounded the ball to Fiore and not Aldridge. Fiore threw the ball to Johnny White, who was at the foul line. As Evansville converged on Johnny White, Aldridge ran in from the corner toward the basket. White turned at the foul line and threw the ball high toward the basket where Aldridge jumped over everyone, caught the ball, and slam dunked it through the basket as time ran out. Castle College had won the Division II National College Championship.

There was bedlam in Burlington. People who had been watching or listening to the game in the bars or in their homes ran out to the streets in jubilation. A Vermont team had won a national championship in a major sport for the first time in history.

When the team returned to the Burlington Airport, they were met by over one thousand jubilant students and fans. Castle College's ROTC band serenaded the entourage of coaches, players, and dignitaries as they disembarked from the airplane.

In the coming weeks, the business community and people of Burlington and the surrounding areas honored the players and coaches with awards and dinners. The players and coaches basked in the glory that they so richly deserved.

Castle College was remembered for their team's tenacity and perseverance while in pursuit of success and in the face of tragedy. Players and coaches would be forever remembered. They were inducted into the Hall of Fame and forever honored for their great deed.

EPILOGUE

The Castle College players were champions in basketball. They were also champions in life.

Hayes Aldridge was named to the All-American NCAA Division II's first team, and he was also drafted by the Boston Celtics. The Celtics were very impressed by Aldridge, but hey had to make him the last cut of the team. They didn't have room for him on their roster. Aldridge decided to put his basketball career on hold. Aldridge, who was a math major, obtained employment at IBM in Essex Junction, Vermont. He gained knowledge about computer systems, which were at their rudimentary beginnings.

When Luke Tate graduated, Aldridge recruited him to also work at IBM. After several years, they started their own company. They used the knowledge that they had learned at IBM to start a computerized billing service for doctors and other professionals. This proved to be such a resounding success that the company spread worldwide.

After thirty years, they were able to sell the company to General Electric for $1 billion and shared the proceeds from the sale. After the sale, Aldridge and Tate became philanthropists, donating money to charities in Vermont. They also gave to Castle College and the University of Vermont.

After his sophomore year and at the urging of Connie Barbeau, Paul Fiore changed his major to education. Paul was much happier with this major and the prospect of teaching in the future. Paul and

Connie both did their practice teaching in Burlington. Paul was certified as a secondary history teacher, and Connie was certified as an elementary teacher.

In his senior year, Paul had become engaged to Connie. After graduation, they moved to Connie's hometown of Newport, Vermont, and they were married.

After several years of teaching in Newport, Paul took a sabbatical and earned a master's degree in administration and supervision at McGill University in Montreal, Canada. He eventually became the superintendent of schools in Newport.

Frank Balboni became a successful insurance executive after working many years for Prudential. Wally Beemer became an assistant coach at Castle College while earning his master's degree. When George Calzoni retired, Joe Mackey became the head coach and retained Beemer as his assistant.

Eventually, Mackey decided to devote all his time to his duties as athletic director and named Beemer head coach. Beemer became a very successful head coach at Castle College for many years and did radio and television commentary for area basketball games.

They were all great basketball players. Their scholarships allowed them to develop their athletic skills, but the education that they received allowed them to become successful professionals and contributors to their communities. The education that they received was as invaluable as their success on the basketball court.

Printed in the United States
by Baker & Taylor Publisher Services